For Lucy, Theo and Tara – PB

For Grace and Rose – FB

STRIPES PUBLISHING
An imprint of Little Tiger Press
1 The Coda Centre, 189 Munster Road,
London SW6 6AW

A paperback original
First published in Great Britain in 2014

Text copyright © Peter Bently, 2014
Illustrations copyright © Fred Blunt, 2014

ISBN: 978-1-84715-449-1

A CIP catalogue record for this book is available from
the British Library.

Printed and bound in the UK.

10 9 8 7 6 5 4 3 2 1

KNIGHTMARE

Damsel Disaster!

PETER BENTLY

Illustrated by Fred Blunt

stripes

CEDRIC'S WORLD

CASTLE BOMBAST

Cedric Thatchbottom (Me!)

Sir Percy the Proud

Patchcoat the Jester

Margaret the Cook

BLACKSTONE FORT

Sir Roland the Rotten

Walter Warthog

SPIFFINGTON MANOR

Algernon Whympleigh

Sir Spencer the Splendid

Chapter One
Tour de Farce

Toot! Toot-TOOT!

Toot! Toot-TOOOOT!

"Ah, there's the post!" said Sir Percy. "Splendid! Run along and fetch it, Cedric."

"Yes, Sir Percy."

I quickly finished strapping the last bit of armour to my master's leg and hurried out of the stables to the castle gate.

KNIGHTMARE

"Mornin', Master Cedric," said the messenger, tucking his posthorn back into his belt. "Sir Percy's popular today."

He handed over a pile of parchment scrolls. A few looked suspiciously like fan mail from Sir Percy's female admirers. One was tied up with pink ribbons. Another had little red love hearts drawn all over it (bleh). But most were bills with things like PAY NOW! and FINAL DEMAND – THIS TIME I REALLY MEAN IT! on them in big red letters.

"Thanks," I said, turning to go.

"Wait, Master Cedric!" the messenger said. "There's this box an' all." He untied a long, polished wooden box from his saddle.

"What is it?" I asked.

"Search me," said the messenger. "Posh box, though, innit?"

I piled the scrolls on top of the box and staggered back to the stables, where my master and I had been preparing to ride off on a tour of his lands. Sir Percy said it was important for a knight to show his face to the locals every now and then. But I reckon he just liked the excuse to show off his best armour. Especially after I'd spent most of the morning polishing it.

"Letters for you, Sir Percy!" I said. "Plus this box."

"Excellent!" said Sir Percy. He carefully picked out the fan mail and then brushed all the bills on to the ground with a majestic sweep of his arm. "I shall – er – *deal* with those later," he said airily.

I watched as Sir Percy eagerly undid the catch on the box. Was it a new sword? Unlikely. The last thing Sir Percy ever spent money on – when he had any – was weapons.

He opened the lid to reveal something long, white and fluffy.

KNIGHTMARE

"Look, Cedric!" beamed Sir Percy, taking it out. "It's my new plume! Magnificent, is it not?"

"A *plume*, Sir Percy?" I said. "You mean those are – *feathers*?"

"Indeed!" said Sir Percy. "They are from a giant bird called an *ostrich*. Terribly rare beast, you know. A sort of cross between a chicken and a giraffe."

KNIGHTMARE

While Sir Percy was admiring his plume I spotted a sheet of parchment in the bottom of the box. At the top of the sheet it said *Pierre de Pompom's Prime Plumes*. Underneath were the words FOR IMMEDIATE PAYMENT next to a *very* large number.

"How fortunate that this should arrive just before our little tour, eh, Cedric?" Sir Percy plucked the plume out of his helmet and fitted the new one. "There." He handed me the old plume. "Kindly return this to my collection."

"Yes, Sir Percy."

As I headed back across the courtyard I bumped into Patchcoat the jester coming out of the castle.

"Morning, Ced!" he chirped. "Where's Sir Percy off to then? And why is he wearing an extra-large feather duster on his head?"

I explained about the new plume.

"*Ostrich?*" said Patchcoat. "Blimey. I bet that cost a bit."

When I told him about the bill, Patchcoat whistled in amazement.

"Phew!" he gasped. "For that price I reckon they should've chucked in the whole ostrich! Well, I dunno how Sir Percy's going to pay for it. Margaret's already moaning about how little he gives her for all the food."

Mouldybun Margaret is the castle cook. And possibly the worst cook in the kingdom, too, though no one would dare to tell her that.

"Anyway," said Patchcoat, "I'd better be off. I'm going for a tinkle."

"Thanks for sharing," I said.

"Not *that* kind of tinkle," chuckled Patchcoat. "I've lost a bell off my cap. I'm nipping to the village for a new one. See ya later, Ced. Have a good tour!"

We set off along the road to the village, Sir Percy looking rather splendid in his freshly polished armour on the back of Prancelot, his haughty horse. I trotted behind him on Gristle the mule.

"Cedric, this tour will be excellent training for when you yourself are a knight," Sir Percy said.

Sir Percy is always promising to teach me real knight stuff but somehow never gets round to it. Riding past a few peasants didn't sound much like knight training. But at least it got me out of chores for a few hours.

A bunch of peasant women on their way to market turned to stare at us as we passed.

"Ooh, look!" cried one. "There goes Sir Percy the Proud!"

"'E's well famous, yer know," said another.

It's true, my master is very famous. Mainly because of his best-selling book, *The Song of Percy*, which is full of all his amazingly brave and dangerous deeds. Like when he single-handedly banished all the dragons in the kingdom to a deep cave in the Mountains of Myrk, wherever that is.

Now, a squire should never be rude about his master. So let's just say that a lot of *The Song of Percy* might be a bit, well, *unreliable*. You see, if Sir Percy has to do anything brave or dangerous he usually gets me to do it for him. Especially if it involves his arch-enemy, Sir Roland the Rotten.

Still, as Sir Percy nodded and smiled at the peasant women he certainly looked the part of the bold and daring knight.

"Ha, Cedric!" he chortled. "If you ever get to be a famous knight such as myself you'll be fending off whole *legions* of ladies!"

"Um, yes, Sir Percy," I said, feeling my face go red.

Sir Percy grinned. "Blushing at the thought of all those lady admirers," he said. "Oh, to be so young and innocent! But let me give you a word of advice, Cedric. Ladies are wonderful creatures, of course, but they're highly *mysterious*, too. Their brains

17

work in *peculiar* ways, you see."

"Really, Sir Percy?" I said.

"Indeed," Sir Percy went on. "I suppose that's why damsels get themselves into distress. But fortunately, there are gallant knights such as myself to rescue them!"

"Yes, Sir Percy."

As we rode on I wondered how long Sir Percy's "tour" was going to last. He was bound to get bored sooner or later. Probably when there was no one else around to show off his new plume to.

I was just thinking that we hadn't met anyone for a while, when a tall young woman in expensive-looking clothes suddenly stepped out of the bushes ahead

of us. Or rather, she *tried* to. Something
held her back. She began to struggle. Then
she cried out. I think it was something
about her dress, but I couldn't quite catch
what she said over the sound of hooves.

"Aha, Cedric, a damsel!" said Sir Percy.
"And did you hear that? She just said she's
in distress!"

"Are you sure, Sir Percy?" I said. "It
sounded more like—"

But Sir Percy cut me off. "Cedric, now
you'll see some *real* knighting skills in
action. Watch and learn!"

Sir Percy galloped on ahead. The young
woman was still struggling to get out of the
bushes as he reached her.

"Fear not, sweet damsel!" cried Sir Percy. "Assistance is at hand!"

"Oh good," said the young woman. "You can help me to— Hey! What the—?"

Before she could say another word, Sir Percy leaned out of the saddle and grabbed her round the waist. I think he was trying to hoist her up on to Prancelot in one swift, elegant move. But it didn't quite work out that way. For a start, the young woman still seemed to be caught on something. Then she began kicking and wriggling. And saying some VERY rude words.

"Fear not, sweet damsel!" said Sir Percy again. "I shall save you!"

He tugged and tugged until— *RRRIP!*

With a shriek the woman shot
skywards. She landed in Sir Percy's arms,
her feet pointing up in the air and her head
dangling near one of his stirrups.

"Eeek!" she screeched from somewhere
inside a tangled mass of petticoats. "What
do you think you're doing?"

"Saving you, sweet damsel!" said

Sir Percy. "You are in distress!"

"You can say that again," snapped the young woman. "Put me down at once!" She pounded Sir Percy's armour with her fists. "Help! Help! I'm being kidnapped! Help!"

"Do be careful, sweet damsel!" cried Sir Percy in alarm. "You'll unbalance— *AAAAAARRGH*!"

Sir Percy lurched sideways to dodge a well-aimed kick from a pointy-toed shoe. Unfortunately he lurched a bit too far. With a loud wail he tumbled off Prancelot into the bushes – taking the young woman with him.

"Ooof!"

"Ouch!"

KNIGHTMARE

I leaped from my saddle.

"Gosh!" I said, pulling the young woman free. "Are you all right, miss?"

"*All right*, boy?" she yelled. "I've just been seized by a raving lunatic and dumped upside down in a bramble bush. Of course I'm not all right!"

Sir Percy struggled to his feet. "But sweet damsel—" he began.

"Oh, stop calling me that, you tin-covered twit!" she raged. "My dress is torn to shreds! At least *you're* wearing armour."

Sir Percy *did* look pretty unscathed. Except, alas, for his expensive new plume. The ostrich feathers were dangling down to his waist, all crumpled and bedraggled.

Chapter Two
Rescue Rumpus

"Well, don't just stand there, you metallic moron!" fumed the young woman. "I demand an explanation!"

Sir Percy stood frozen to the spot with his mouth open. But at last he managed to speak. "Well, sweet – er – dear lady," he gabbled. "I – I – that is to say, um – um – *my squire* here saw you struggling in the bushes. I – er – I mean *he* distinctly heard you crying out that you were *in distress.* Isn't that right, Cedric?"

"Oh – er – yes," I said. *You definitely owe me one, Sir Percy!* I thought.

"You see, my lady?" he continued. "And of course the moment he told me *that,* I rode to your aid at once like the dutiful knight that I am!"

"You pair of dunderbrains!" she cried. "I didn't say anything about being *in distress.* I said, 'I wish I hadn't come out *in this dress.'* I was cross because I'd caught it on the brambles. I thought you were coming to help me pull it free. But now you've *totally* ruined it, Sir – Sir—"

KNIGHTMARE

"Er – *Patrick*," said Sir Percy. "My dear lady, you have been the victim of a most unfortunate error. I do hope you will accept—"

"The money for a new dress?" she said.

"Er – *my squire's* apologies," said Sir Percy.

I bowed and looked suitably sheepish. "Sorry, miss," I said.

KNIGHTMARE

"My lady," said Sir Percy. "Now that's all cleared up I trust you will allow me to escort you home."

"Home?" said the young woman. "Not likely. My home is many miles away and I don't think I could put up with you for that long. However, you *can* escort me back to where I'm staying tonight. It's a horrid little inn down the road. The Bear's Bellybutton or something."

"Oh, you mean the Boar's Bottom?" I piped up.

"That's the one," she said with a shudder. "The whole place positively *reeks* of peasant. That's why I nipped out in the first place. For a bit of fresh air."

KNIGHTMARE

Sir Percy put his foot in one of Prancelot's stirrups. But the young woman stood in his way.

"What are you doing?" she said. "Surely you don't think I'm going to walk? I shall ride your horse, Sir Patrick."

"But – but – what about me?" said Sir Percy.

"Well, I'm sure your squire won't mind giving up his mount for his master."

"But – but – my lady!" spluttered Sir Percy. "I can't ride a *mule*."

"Really?" said the young woman. "I'm sure it's just the same as riding a horse."

I tried not to smile.

"No, I mean – it's – it's terribly

undignified," said Sir Percy.

"Suit yourself," said the young woman. "You'll just have to run alongside me. I hope you can keep up!" She skilfully swung herself up on to Prancelot, who snorted in protest. "And I'll have no moaning from you, you old nag. Giddy up!"

Prancelot reluctantly started to trot away. Sir Percy stood there, not sure what to do.

The woman swung round in the saddle. "Come along, Sir Patrick," she barked.

"Er – at once, my lady!" he replied. "Cedric, help me up."

Gristle had no stirrups so I gave Sir Percy a leg-up into the saddle. The mule brayed grumpily at the extra weight.

29

KNIGHTMARE

"A knight on a mule! Oh, the humiliation!" muttered Sir Percy, grabbing the reins. "I only hope no one sees me. Thank goodness the inn isn't far. Now gee up, or whatever it is one says to mules."

Gristle's idea of geeing up was to bray crossly and kick out his hind legs – nearly tipping off Sir Percy in the process. Then he started to walk *very* slowly. Sir Percy tried his best to look noble and dignified.

Which wasn't easy with a tattered plume flopping about his shoulders.

KNIGHTMARE

I watched until Sir Percy disappeared round the bend in the road. A couple of minutes later, a laughing crowd of peasants came past. It didn't take long to find out what was so funny.

"Fancy seein' Sir Percy on a mule!" said one.

"Arrr!" cackled another. "And what was that on 'is 'ead? Looked like a bunch o' dead chickens!"

The crowd roared with laughter as they went off down the road. Then I spotted someone else coming round the corner, whistling. It was Patchcoat.

KNIGHTMARE

"Wotcher, Ced!" he called. "What's going on? I was just leaving the shop with my new bell and saw Sir Percy outside the Boar's Bottom. This tall posh lady was giving him a right old earful."

I told Patchcoat what had happened.

"What a hoot!" he chortled. "Anyhow, talking of posh ladies, take a look at this poster. It was stuck on a tree near the inn."

He took out a scroll of parchment from his jerkin and unrolled it.

Her Royal Highness Princess Astra-Felicia seeks a HUSBAND. Must be a brave and intelligent knight. Good looks a bonus.

Knights must arrive at NOMAN CASTLE on Ladyburg Lake, Saturday at midday sharp, to take part in a CHALLENGE. No fops, fools, freaks or flatterers. (Or peasants. Obviously.)

"Isn't Princess Astra-Fer-whatsit from the kingdom next door?" I asked. "She's got a holiday castle not far from here. I think my dad went there once to fix a leaky roof."

"That's right," said Patchcoat. "The castle's on an island next to the town of Ladyburg, a few hours' ride from here. I went to a joke contest there once – The

33

Ladyburg Jest Fest. It was a right hoot."
He sighed. "Didn't win, mind."

"Look, there's a mistake in the poster,"
I said. "Shouldn't that be *Norman* Castle?"

Patchcoat shook his head. "Oh no, Ced.
There's no mistake," he said. "Apparently
it's called Noman Castle because *no man* is
allowed to set foot in it."

"Gosh, Saturday's tomorrow!" I said.
"Anyway, I don't know if Sir Percy even
wants to get married. What makes you
think he'd be interested?"

"Interested in what, dear boy?" said a
voice.

We looked up. It was Sir Percy. He
was back on Prancelot and leading

Gristle by the reins.

I showed him the poster.

"Pah!" huffed Sir Percy. "I've had quite enough of dealing with ladies for one day, thank you very much. The last thing I want to do is marry some bossy princess. Come along, Cedric. I'm going back to Castle Bombast for a lie-down."

With that he began to ride on.

"Oh well, never mind," sighed Patchcoat, turning to me. "Sir Percy's right. She probably *is* a bit bossy. Fabulously rich princesses often are."

Sir Percy stopped. He slowly turned in his saddle. A smile spread over his face. "On the other hand, dear boy…"

Chapter Three
Peasant Palaver

The next morning the castle clock was
striking ten as Sir Percy, Patchcoat and I
all set off for Noman Castle. As usual Sir
Percy rode in front while Patchcoat and I
followed in the cart pulled by Gristle. We
were just heading through the castle gate
when Mouldybun Margaret came running
after us.

KNIGHTMARE

"Wait, Master Cedric!" she cried. "I've made Sir Percy a packed lunch. A lovely pie, fresh out the oven!" She handed me a cloth bundle tied up with string. It was warm and steaming and stank like a cross between boiled cabbage and a blocked drain. With a sort of fishy whiff thrown in.

"Thanks, Margaret," I said. "What is it? It smells – um – *interesting.*"

"It's one of me noo budget recipes," said Margaret proudly. "Snake and kidney pie. I had to change it a bit, mind. The butcher swore them kidneys was only a week old, but it turns out they was off."

"No *way*," said Patchcoat, pretending to sound surprised.

"Aye," said Margaret, giving him a beady stare.

"So I chucked in a few old fish heads to disguise the smell. Took me ages to find 'em. They was right at the bottom of the slop bucket."

"Er, thanks, Margaret," I said queasily. I stuffed the bundle into my saddlebag.

"Yum!" said Patchcoat, as we rode on. "Lucky Sir Percy!"

A couple of hours later we were riding up a long, wooded hill in a part of the country I didn't know.

KNIGHTMARE

"Not much further now, chaps," called Sir Percy cheerfully, as we passed a signpost that said LADYBURG 5 MILES.

I turned to Patchcoat. "I wonder what the challenge will be."

"No idea," said Patchcoat. "But I'm surprised Sir Percy sounds so jolly. If there's a test of bravery you'd think he'd be getting a bit nervous by now. I wonder if he's up to something."

Hmm. It was true. Whatever it said in *The Song of Percy*, my master normally tried to wriggle out of anything that was actually dangerous. Could he be planning to cheat? It didn't take long to find out.

"Cedric," said Sir Percy. "I trust you have *The Song of Percy* in your saddlebag?"

"Of course, Sir Percy," I said.

"Excellent," said Sir Percy. "The moment we meet the princess I will simply slip her my book. She will read it and see at once that I am the suitor for her. Although of course she probably has a copy already. Pass it here, would you, Cedric?"

I opened my saddlebag and took out the small leather-bound book. As I handed it over a sharp pong from inside the bag reminded me of Margaret's pie.

"Oh, Sir Percy," I said. "I forgot to mention – Margaret's made you a pie."

"Goody!" said Sir Percy. "Kindly pass

it over. I'm ravenous!"

I gave Sir Percy the cloth bundle.

"Um – rather interesting *aroma*, Cedric," he said, unwrapping the pie. "What's in it?"

"It's Margaret's own – er – special recipe, Sir Percy," I said.

Sir Percy hungrily wolfed down a huge chunk. As he swallowed it he went cross-eyed and gave a shudder. He tried to speak but all that came out was "*Whauugh!*" "*Eeeesh!*" and "*Gaaah!*"

"Are you all right, Sir Percy?" I asked.

He belched very loudly. A foul blast of cabbagey-sewery-fishy breath blew over me and Patchcoat.

"Pardon me!" gasped Sir Percy. "Gosh! Well, that's – er – certainly cured my appetite, Cedric." He passed me the pie. "Here. You're – um – most welcome to finish it. One doesn't like to be *greedy*."

"Er – thanks, Sir Percy," I said, stuffing what was left of the pie back in my saddlebag. "I'll save it for later."

KNIGHTMARE

As we neared the top of the hill, a rather ominous glooping and gurgling noise started to come from Sir Percy's tummy. It got louder and louder. And then Sir Percy began making some *other* very loud noises, too. Let's just say Patchcoat and I were glad the breeze was coming from behind us.

We reached the crest of the hill. About a mile ahead, down in a broad valley, a jumble of roofs and spires peeped up over the walls of a small town.

"That's Ladyburg right in front of us!" called Patchcoat.

Ladyburg stood on the shores of a wide lake. From the island in the middle of the lake rose a castle. It was surrounded by

43

trees and its six tall pointy towers glistened in the sunshine.

"And that must be Noman Castle," I said.

"Marvellous!" said Sir Percy. "We should easily get there by midday."

But as we headed down the hill we saw that the road in front of us was crowded with men all the way to the gates of the town.

"Excuse me, gentlemen," called Sir Percy, as we came to the back of the line. "Kindly let me past. I have – er – important business at the castle."

The man at the end of the line turned round. He was wearing a cracked old chamber pot on his head.

"The castle, eh?" he said. "Yer better join the queue then, mate, 'adn't yer?"

"Queue?" Sir Percy puffed out his chest. "My dear sir, I will have you know that I am riding to see Her Royal Highness Princess Fel – Astral— *OOOH!*"

Sir Percy groaned as his tummy gave its loudest grumble so far.

"Astra-Felicia, Sir Percy," I said.

"Precisely, Cedric," said Sir Percy, recovering. "And I'll have you know, sir, that I have every intention of becoming her husband!"

Chamber-pot man roared with laughter and several other men turned round.

They were also wearing pots and buckets on their heads.

"'Ear that, lads?" said chamber-pot man. "We're all wastin' our time! This joker reckons she's already chosen *'im*!"

The men nearby tittered.

"Just cos 'e's splashed out on a proper knight's costoom," jeered a man squinting out from a hole in the side of a rotten old bucket.

KNIGHTMARE

"How rude!" said Sir Percy. "Don't you— *OOOH!*" He grimaced as his tummy gave an even louder grumble. "Don't you know who you're talking to?"

Chamber-pot man screwed up his eyes and stared closely at Sir Percy. Then he grinned.

"Arrr! Of course!" he declared. "You're that ratcatcher from up Little Piddlington way."

"I – *ooooh!* – most certainly am not!" snorted Sir Percy. "My dear sir, I am a *real* knight. In fact, I am none other than Sir Percy the Proud!"

"Arr, me, too!" said a man sporting a battered old sieve with a leafy twig stuck in the top. "Do 'ee like me plume?"

"An' I'm Sir Roland the Rotten!" said the man in the holey bucket. He lifted it to reveal a moustache made out of straw and tied under his nose with string.

"So yer see, mister, we're *all* waiting to see the princess," said chamber-pot man. "Yer'll just have to join the queue."

"Oh, Cedric, this is ridiculous!" said Sir Percy. "I refuse to be held up by a crowd of peasants shamelessly pretending to be knights. It's against the law, for one thing. It's also jolly unfair. I do hate cheating."

Yeah, right, I thought.

"It's nearly midday and they're going to make me late. Cedric, please get rid of them and— *OOOOH! AAAAH!* Oh dear. I think I'm going to … I need… Oh no. *ARRRGH!* GET OUT OF MY WAY!"

In a flash Sir Percy slid off Prancelot and bolted into the woods, clutching his tummy.

"Where's 'e off to then?" asked chamber-pot man.

"Oh, he's given up and gone home," said Patchcoat.

"Huh?" I began. But Patchcoat quickly dug me in the ribs.

"He knew that costume of his wouldn't fool anyone," Patchcoat went on. "You see, it's only made of shiny paper."

What on earth was Patchcoat playing at?

"Arr, I could tell!" said chamber-pot man. "Looks right cheap 'n' nasty!"

"Yeah, doesn't it?" chuckled Patchcoat. "Not like that helmet you've got there. That looks *really* fireproof."

"Eh?" said chamber-pot man. "What d'yer mean, fireproof?"

"Well, it'll be useful when you fight the dragon," said Patchcoat.

"Dragon? What dragon?" said chamber-pot man.

Aha. *Now* I saw what Patchcoat was up to. But would they believe him?

At that moment there was a tremendous exploding noise from the nearby woods, accompanied by a wild, blood-curdling howl.

"*WAAAARRGGGGH!!!*"

The crowd shuffled nervously.

"*That* dragon," said Patchcoat. "You know, the one the princess has got chained up in the woods."

There was another thunderous explosion and an even more terrifying howl.

"'Ere – that there poster only says

51

there'll be a challenge. It don't say nothin'
about fightin' no dragons!" said the man
in the holey bucket.

There were murmurs of agreement.

Patchcoat hesitated.

"Um – of course not," I piped up.
"There's no need. *Real* knights don't mind
what challenges they face. Fighting a
terrifying fire-breathing dragon? That's all
in a day's work for a *real* knight."

"Er, yeah! That's right," smiled
Patchcoat. "But don't worry, lads. Those
helmets of yours should last a good few
seconds before you're burned to a crisp."

More mutterings among the crowd
were interrupted by a third resounding

blast and the most terrifying roar yet.

"That does it," said chamber-pot man in alarm. "I'm not ending up a dragon's cooked breakfast, princess or no princess!"

"Nor me neither," said holey bucket man shakily. "If I gets eaten by a dragon me mum'll kill me! I'm off!"

They hurried past us up the road.

"Wait for me!" said the man in the sieve.

KNIGHTMARE

News of the dragon spread along the queue like wildfire (or maybe that should be dragonfire). Before long the crowd was fleeing like a flock of frightened chickens.

Patchcoat and I collapsed in fits of giggles as another explosion from the trees sent the last stragglers scuttling up the road.

"Thanks for helping me out there," grinned Patchcoat. "For a second I thought they weren't going to buy it."

"No probs," I said. "What gave you the genius idea about the dragon?"

"It's all down to Sir Percy, really. I once made the mistake of eating one of Margaret's budget pies. I recognized the signs. Once he dashed off into the woods it was just a question of timing."

There was a clanking sound as Sir Percy staggered from the trees, fiddling with the straps of his thigh armour.

"That's better," he said. "Cedric, give me a hand, will you? Can't seem to get these wretched bits back on."

It wasn't really surprising, seeing as he'd got the armour upside down.

"Excellent!" said Sir Percy, as I helped him with the straps. "I see the queue has disappeared."

"Yes, Sir Percy," I said. "It was brilliant! You see, Patchcoat—"

"Brilliant?" he interrupted. "I'm sure

it was, dear boy. I only wish I had seen the faces of those silly peasants when they finally realized that they didn't stand a chance against a *genuine* knight."

"Er, well—" I began. But Sir Percy didn't seem to be listening.

"Onward, Cedric, onward!" he declared, remounting Prancelot. "With no other suitors in sight the princess's hand is as good as mine!"

But at that very moment we heard the sound of hooves. We turned to see two figures galloping up the road towards us. Sir Percy didn't exactly look pleased when he realized that it was none other than his friend Sir Spencer the Splendid and his squire, Algernon.

"Whoa! Hey there, Perce!" called Sir Spencer, his blue-and-gold velvet cloak billowing out behind him. He pulled up alongside us and took off his helmet. "Hope I'm not too late for the princess. Got a bit held up by a whole crowd of peasants going the other way. They kept jabbering on about dragons, didn't they, Algie?"

"Y-yes, Sir Spencer," said Algernon nervously. "There aren't *really* any d-dragons are there, Sir Spencer?"

"Course not!" guffawed Sir Spencer. "Haven't you read *The Song of Percy?* Sir Percy got rid of them all, didn't you, Perce?"

Sir Spencer winked at Sir Percy and clapped him on the back so heartily that his visor clanked shut. "So, Perce, you're after this princess, too, eh?"

"Well, yes," grumbled Sir Percy, lifting his visor again. "As a matter of fact I am."

The clock on the town church struck half past eleven.

"Well, we'd better get this show on the

road then, hadn't we?" said Sir Spencer. "We've got half an hour to get across to that castle. And then we shall just have to see who the princess chooses."

He shook back his long, golden locks.

"Ooh, she's bound to choose *you*, Sir Spencer," gushed Algernon.

Sir Spencer flashed his almost-full set of teeth. "Why thank you, Algie," he said. "But I mustn't be unfair to my pal Percy here. Though of course if he *does* lose, at least he's brought his jester to cheer him up, eh, Perce?"

"Ha ha ha!" said Sir Percy. "*Most* amusing, Spence!" He was grinning so widely it looked like his face would crack.

Chapter Four

Potion Commotion

"Bother!" whispered Sir Percy, as we all rode through the town gates together. "Why did Spencer have to show up? I'll have to think of some new way of winning the princess."

"But Sir Percy," I said. "What about your book?"

"Ah, um – yes – well," said Sir Percy.

KNIGHTMARE

He seemed slightly embarrassed as he reached into his gauntlet and pulled out *The Song of Percy*. Or rather what was left of it, which was basically just the front and back covers.

"Gosh!" I exclaimed. "What's happened to all the pages? It looks like someone's torn them out!"

"Indeed, dear boy, indeed," he said with a sigh. "Unfortunately when I was recently – er – called into the woods for – um – an urgent *sitting*, I fear I had no suitable *materials* with which to – um – bring my, ahem, *business* to – um – to a proper *conclusion*. First of all I was obliged to use my pants. But they weren't quite – erm

61

– up to the job. That's when I remembered my book."

He looked sadly at the cover.

"Ah," I said. "Oh dear." I didn't ask him where he'd left his pants.

"Hey, Perce," called Sir Spencer. "Any idea how we get to that island?"

"Er, no," said Sir Percy.

"I think the jetty is this way," said Patchcoat, pointing down a street to our left. "We should be able to get a boat from there."

"Ah yes, I was forgetting you've been here before," said Sir Percy. "Local knowledge, eh?"

"Not really," smiled Patchcoat. "I just

read the sign."

The sign read "Jetty Lane".

At that moment there was a loud
BANG from a rickety old house just in
front of us. Our animals whinnied in alarm
and Algernon squealed in terror. A few
seconds later, the door of the house burst
open and a man in a crumpled pointed hat
came running out in a big smelly cloud
of yellow smoke. He was coughing and
spluttering and flapping his arms wildly.

"Good grief, man!" cried Sir Percy. "You frightened the living daylights out of us. What's going on? Are you all right?"

"Apologies, apologies!" wheezed the man. "Nothing to be alarmed about, gentlemen! I think I added a bit too much sulphur. I shall have to tweak the formula yet again. Right. Back to work for me. Good day, gentlemen!" With that he scuttled back into his house.

"What a funny chap," I said. "And what was all that about a formula?"

"I think he's an alchemist," said Patchcoat. "It's a sort of inventor. They're always making weird potions and mucking about with chemicals."

KNIGHTMARE

"Really? Weird potions, eh?" said Sir Percy. He narrowed his eyes and stroked his chin. "Hmm… I wonder," he muttered. Then suddenly he leaped down from Prancelot and strode towards the alchemist's door.

"Hey, Perce, where are you going?" said Sir Spencer. "We don't want to be late for the princess!"

"Don't worry, I'll be back in a tick!" Sir Percy said cheerfully. "I just want to see if this alchemist fellow has – er – any potions for – for tummy trouble."

A few minutes later Sir Percy came back out of the house carrying two small bottles of liquid. He remounted

Prancelot, stuffed one bottle in his saddlebag and uncorked the other.

"No time like the present," he said, swigging the contents in one gulp. He pulled a face. "Ugh! Tastes ghastly. Must be those dried toads' eyes that chap put in. But he said my tummy should be right as rain in an hour or two."

As we headed off down Jetty Lane, I turned to Patchcoat. "I suppose that's why the alchemist gave him two bottles," I said. "Just in case one isn't enough."

"Maybe," said Patchcoat. "Except

KNIGHTMARE

that the potion he just drank was green.
The other stuff was *red*. I wonder what Sir
Percy's up to."

We came to the shore of the lake and
saw three people standing next to a large
rowing boat. One was a peasant wearing a
basket on his head. The other two were a
knight and his squire on horseback. They
looked all too familiar.

Sir Percy groaned. My heart sank.

"Well, don't say I didn't warn yer!" the
peasant was saying. "There be dragons!
'Undreds of 'em! That there princess feeds
'em knights fer breakfast!"

"Blithering broadswords!" roared
the knight. "Dragons don't exist, you

67

pea-brained peasant. And even if they did, they'd be too terrified to come anywhere near *ME*!"

In front of us stood the nastiest knight in the kingdom, Sir Roland the Rotten, and his sneaky squire, Walter Warthog.

"Ah, good morning, Sir Roland," said Sir Percy. "How *delightful* to see you here."

"Well, well, well," sneered Walter, as we rode up to the jetty. "If it isn't peasant-features Fatbottom himself."

KNIGHTMARE

Walter always likes to remind me that my mum and dad aren't posh like his.

"Hello, *Wartface*," I said.

Sir Roland glared at Sir Percy and Sir Spencer. "What the blazes are *you* two doing here?" he growled.

Before the other knights could answer, the town clock struck midday. A pair of identical twin sisters emerged from a little cottage next to the jetty. They rolled up their sleeves to reveal arms like enormous hams.

"You gents wanting a boat to the castle?" asked one.

"Why, yes," said Sir Percy.

"Right then, off yer 'orses!" said her sister. "Stables is through there."

KNIGHTMARE

Walter, Algernon and I tied up the animals, then we accompanied our masters on to the boat. Sir Roland barged ahead to grab the seat at the bow. Algernon would probably have fallen overboard if Sir Spencer hadn't grabbed him by the leg at the last moment.

"Oi! Stop that!" bellowed one of the sisters as the ferry wobbled alarmingly. "You'll tip us all out!"

KNIGHTMARE

"Oh dear, Sir Spencer," whined Algernon. "I'm feeling a bit seasick."

The sisters sat down and grabbed a huge oar each. Then, without the slightest effort, they began to row us across the lake.

As we got closer to the island the castle rose up before us. Waiting on the opposite jetty stood a richly dressed aristocratic lady. She looked rather stern. She was also about as old and wrinkly as my granny.

I saw the three knights exchange glances.

"Funny," said Patchcoat. "I'd heard the princess was a lot younger."

"Mind you, it doesn't actually *mention* her age on the poster, does it?" I said.

"Come, come now, Cedric," said Sir Percy. "A true knight does not judge a lady by her age. He prefers nobler qualities such as intelligence and wit and – and…"

A coffer full of cash, I thought.

There was a slight bump as the sisters brought us in to the jetty.

"Right, boys, out you get!" they hollered.

KNIGHTMARE

The knights stepped out of the ferry first. They approached the aristocratic lady and removed their helmets.

Sir Percy made a very elaborate bow. "Your Royal Highness," he said. "Sir Percy the Proud, at your service!"

The lady gave a start of surprise.

"What?" she said. "I'm not the princess, you fool! Her Royal Highness is inside the castle. I am the Countess Sendham-Packing. But you may address me as High Steward."

"Hi, Stewart!" beamed Sir Spencer. "Cool name for a lady!"

The countess glared at him so fiercely that he gave a little squeak.

"You hare-brained clothes-horse!" she hissed. "I am the *High Steward* of Noman Castle. I look after Her Royal Highness and make sure everything runs smoothly. It is also my job to keep out revolting peasants and –" she looked at the three knights in turn – "*other* undesirables. Now, you'd better follow me and prepare yourselves."

"To meet the princess?" said Sir Roland. "About bloomin' time!"

"What?" snapped the High Steward. "Don't be ridiculous. You read the poster. Before you meet Her Royal Highness you will all be put to the test. She is only interested in knights who are *intelligent* and *brave*."

"And *handsome?*" piped up Sir Spencer feebly. The High Steward shot him a look that could pierce a hole in armour.

"*Intelligent* and *brave*," the High Steward repeated. "Of course it's easy for someone to *say* they're brave and intelligent, isn't it? But for all we know they might just be making it up."

Maybe it was a trick of the light, but I could have sworn that for a split second the High Steward glanced at Sir Percy. He smiled rather feebly.

"Let us waste no more time," the High Steward went on. "Knights, follow me and prepare to face your challenge!"

Chapter Five
Loo Hullaballoo

The High Steward led the way. The castle was surrounded by trees except for a broad lawn next to the lake. In the centre stood a large pavilion.

"D'you reckon Sir Percy's all right, Ced?" asked Patchcoat. "He still looks a bit peaky."

"I know," I said. "I don't think the

tummy potion has started working yet."

As if to prove it, Sir Percy's tummy gave a very loud gloop.

"Oh dear," he grimaced. "I-I think I might need to visit the – er – you know, the – um – *garderobe*."

"Poor Percy-wercy needs a poop!" roared Sir Roland. "HUR-HUR … um, hur."

The High Steward silenced him with a glare. "Oh, for goodness' sake, Sir Percy," she snapped. "Why didn't you go before you came?"

"Um – as a matter of fact I *did*, Your Stewardship," said Sir Percy. "*Ooooh!* I can't … hold on … much longer!"

"Oh, very well," she sighed. "You can use the servants' privy in the kitchens, through there." She nodded to a small archway. "But you must NOT set foot anywhere else in the castle, is that clear? Any knight who enters the castle without permission will be instantly disqualified!"

"Y-yes, Your Stewardship," said Sir Percy. "Come along, Cedric, hurry!"

"Me, Sir Percy?" I said.

"Of course, dear boy!" he groaned, gripping his tummy. "I shall need you … *oooh!* … to help with my straps. Quickly— *Oooh!*"

I sprinted ahead of Sir Percy. I reached the archway first, ran into the kitchen yard – and tripped over a large goat.

"BEEEHH!"

"Waah!"

Luckily I had a soft (though rather smelly) landing in a large pile of vegetable peelings. But no sooner had I hauled myself to my knees than the grumpy goat went "BEEEHH!" again and gave me a sharp butt in the backside.

KNIGHTMARE

"Ouch!" I cried, sprawling headlong back into the slippery heap.

"Shoo, Stewie, shoo!" said a voice.

I looked up to see a girl of about my age shoving the goat out of the way.

"Sorry!" she giggled. "Stewie's a sweetie really. It's just that you're lying on his dinner, see."

"Ugh!" I grimaced. I stood up and brushed off the worst of the muck.

"Hello, I'm Peggy," smiled the girl. "Who are you? We don't get many boys round 'ere. Actually we don't get *any*."

"Er, I'm Cedric," I said. My face felt quite hot. Probably from all that running. "I'm with my master. He desperately needs—"

80

KNIGHTMARE

And then Sir Percy himself hurtled into the yard, bent double and clutching his grumbling guts.

"THE LOO, CEDRIC, THE LOO, QUICKLY! *OOOOH!*"

"Gosh!" gasped Peggy. "A real knight! But men ain't allowed in the castle!"

"It's all right," I said. "The High Steward said he can use the servants' privy."

"Oh, in that case follow me, sir."

Peggy led us inside and threw open a small door just off the kitchen. It was full of row upon row of expensive-looking dresses.

"But … this isn't … a loo*OOOOOH*!" protested Sir Percy.

"Yes 'tis, sir!" said Peggy. "Just go through. Loo's at the far end."

Peggy waited outside while Sir Percy and I fumbled our way past the rows of dresses. The place certainly *smelled* like a loo. And there at the end of the room was a plank with a hole in it.

"Thank goodness!" grimaced Sir Percy. "My armour, Cedric! Hurry! *Oooh!*"

I hastily untied the straps of his leg armour.

"Thank you," he grunted. "Now GO!"

I hurried out of the servants' privy and shut the door just before a barrage of explosions.

"Oo-er! Sounds bad!" said Peggy. "Whassamatter with your master?"

"Something he ate," I said. "So what's with all the posh frocks in the privy?"

"They're Her Royal Highness's best dresses," said Peggy. "She reckons the smell keeps off the moths, so she keeps 'em in there. Much smellier than her own privy cos all us servants use it, see. Anyway, I'd best get back to work. I've got to pick some lemons for the princess's lemonade. She always has lemonade in the afternoon. If old Stewie catches me chattin' she'll kill me!"

"What?" I said. "Stewie the goat?"

"No, Stewie the High Steward," she sniggered. "Goat's named after 'er. Don't tell, will you?"

"Course not!" I grinned.

"Ta! Bye then, Cedric," said Peggy. "See you later, I hope!"

She smiled and gave me a little wave as she left the kitchen. My face felt hot again. Probably because of the kitchen fire. Yes, that's it. Definitely the fire.

After a while the explosions stopped and Sir Percy called me to help him put his armour back on. As I entered the privy I tried my hardest not to breathe. I won't go into detail. Let's just say there was no chance of the princess's clothes being eaten by moths any time soon.

We returned to Patchcoat and the others in the clearing by the lake. We were just in time to hear Sir Roland and Walter starting to chant, "*Why are we waiting? Why-y are we waiting?*"

"Silence!" cried the High Steward.

"There you are, Sir Percy. About time, too. Are you feeling better?"

"Ah, yes, thank you, I—"

"Good!" she cut him short. "Now, gentlemen, your challenge is to rescue a lady from captivity. Only those who pass the test will be permitted to meet the princess!"

"Excellent, Cedric!" said Sir Percy. "A *genuine* damsel in distress. Splendid! This time you'll *really* see how it's done. So, Your Stewardship, where is this damsel? Tied up somewhere among these trees?"

"No," said the High Steward. "Up there." She pointed to the tall, round tower behind her. Perched on the battlements, about thirty feet off the ground, were three stuffed dummies.

"What?" protested Sir Roland. "Aren't we going to rescue the real princess?"

"Don't be ridiculous," snorted the High Steward. "Do you think Her Highness would be stupid enough to put herself at risk?"

"Well, at least we won't have to worry about any kicking and screaming," said Sir Percy. "So all we have to do is run to the top of the tower, grab a dummy and run down. The fastest knight wins, isn't that right, Your Stewardship? Good job I'm not on the porky side, eh, Cedric?" he smirked. "I reckon *some people* would have a job making it up all those stairs!"

KNIGHTMARE

He glanced slyly at Sir Roland.

Sir Roland glared back. "Right, Percy," he growled. "Just you wait—"

"Silence!" barked the High Steward. "Sir Percy, you haven't listened to a word I've said, you cloth-eared clot. I told you before that men are *forbidden* to go inside the castle. That includes the tower."

"But my dear lady," said Sir Percy. "If we can't use the stairs how can we rescue the dummies?"

"Simple," said the High Steward. "From the outside."

Chapter Six

Dummy Trouble

The tower had no windows or ledges and just a few arrow slits near the top. Its stone sides looked as smooth as glass. It would be impossible to climb them unaided.

Sir Percy went rather pale. Sir Spencer, on the other hand, turned positively green.

"W-whaaat?" he squeaked. "You don't mean – c-climb up there?"

"Of course," said the High Steward. "This is a test of *bravery*. Don't tell me you're afraid of heights, Sir Spencer?"

"This isn't terribly *fair*, you know," said Sir Percy. "None of us have brought any equipment. We can hardly climb up with our bare hands, can we?"

"Of course not," snapped the High Steward. "There's plenty of equipment in the pavilion. You can use whatever you like as long as no other knight has chosen it. You will have one attempt only. So what you choose and how you use it will be an *excellent* test of your intelligence."

"Oh, that's all right then," said Sir Percy. "Cedric, there's bound to be a ladder. You can hold it steady while I nip up and rescue—"

"Wait!" said the High Steward. "Each knight must perform the challenge alone. Anyone helped by his squire will be instantly disqualified! Now, gentlemen, let's see who's going first. Pick a ball."

She took a silk pouch from her belt and held it open. Each knight put in his hand and took out a little silver ball with a number on it. Sir Roland chose the number one, Sir Spencer two and Sir Percy three.

"Sir Roland, you're first," said the High Steward. "Choose your equipment."

"Good luck, Sir Roland," smarmed Walter.

"*Luck?* I don't need luck to prove who's the best knight around here!"

Sir Roland went into the pavilion. He came out carrying a rope with a heavy three-pronged hook on the end.

"This will do the job," he said. "Stand back!"

We all scuttled away to a safe distance as Sir Roland started to swing the hook round his head. Then, with a mighty roar, he let go of the rope. The hook hurtled to the top of the tower, caught the edge of the battlements – and stayed there.

"Right, up we go!" laughed Sir Roland. After a quick tug to check the hook was secure, he shinned up the rope like a

squirrel up a tree. We watched in awe
as he reached the battlements, slung the
dummy over his shoulder and shinned
down the rope again at incredible speed.

Sir Roland jumped the last few feet to the ground.

"Hur-hur! I haven't had this much fun since my last siege!" He laughed and flung the dummy to the floor.

"Really, Sir Roland!" snapped the High Steward. "Is that any way to treat a *lady*? I shall bear that in mind in the event of a tie."

Sir Roland looked a bit sheepish.

"Don't worry, Sir Roland, you're still bound to win," said Walter. He turned to me and hissed, "I'd like to see your useless master do better than *that*, Fatbottom!"

"Yikes," I whispered to Patchcoat. "Walter's right. Sir Roland's going to

94

take some beating!"

"Sir Spencer," said the High Steward. "Your turn next!"

Sir Spencer looked frantically around as if he was trying to find a way to escape.

"Come along, Sir Spencer!" barked the High Steward. "We haven't got all day!"

Sir Spencer smiled feebly and finally entered the pavilion. We heard him give a cry of surprise. A few seconds later he came out, dragging a very long ladder behind him.

"Look what I found!" he said. "A siege ladder! You missed a trick there, Roly. Surprised you didn't spot it! This is by far the easiest way to climb a tower, eh, Algie?"

"Oh, well done, Sir Spencer!" beamed Algernon. "You *are* clever!"

I was sure Sir Roland would say something rude. But to my surprise he just smiled.

"Yeah, *really* well done, Spencer," he said. "How very *silly* of me not to use the ladder, eh?"

He sounded sincere – which instantly made me suspicious. Had Sir Roland done something to the ladder?

With much grunting, Sir Spencer lifted the ladder against the tower. It reached just to the battlements.

"Right," he said. "Here goes!"

He muttered something about being

fine as long as he didn't look down. Then, slowly and nervously, he began to climb.

Gradually Sir Spencer got closer and closer to the top. Only a few rungs to go and he'd be within reach of the dummy. But suddenly the ladder gave an ominous creak. Sir Spencer squealed.

"Go on, Sir Spencer," bleated Algernon. "You can do it!"

Sir Spencer grinned faintly. He carefully put his foot on the next rung and hauled himself up.

CRACK!

The rung snapped in two. Sir Spencer's legs flailed about in mid-air as he clung on for dear life. The ladder wobbled horribly.

"Waaah!" Sir Spencer wailed in terror.

"Hey, Spencer," called Sir Roland.
"I forgot to mention why I didn't choose
the ladder. It's riddled with woodworm!
Hur-hur-hur!"

At last the ladder stopped wobbling.

KNIGHTMARE

Very slowly, Sir Spencer began to climb
the last couple of rungs to the battlements.

We watched with bated breath.

Algernon was so nervous he started
jiggling up and down like he desperately
needed a wee.

At last Sir Spencer reached the top. He
clung on to the ladder with one hand and
quickly grabbed a dummy with the other.

"Oh, bravo, Sir Spencer!" cried
Algernon. "I knew you'd do it!"

"N-no problemo!" Sir Spencer called.
"B-back in a jiffy!"

He was holding the dummy rather
awkwardly round the waist and, as
he climbed down, the dummy's head

walloped each rung with a *thonk*. Before long I noticed a small white cloud around Sir Spencer.

"Are those feathers?" I said, turning to Patchcoat.

"Looks like it," he replied. "I think the stuffing's coming out of the dummy."

Sir Spencer suddenly stopped.

"Bother!" he called. "I think I'm going to snee-ee-ee-ah-ah-*A-TISHOO*!"

With the force of the sneeze Sir Spencer flew backwards, yanking the ladder away from the wall again so that it stood dead upright. At the same time, there was a horrible splitting and cracking sound as Sir Spencer slid down several rungs, snapping each one as he went.

The ladder swayed. It teetered. It tottered. For a few seconds it looked like it would just drop back against the wall. But no. We gasped as it began to tilt in the direction of … the lake!

"Algie!" wailed Sir Spencer. "Do something!"

Algernon ran to the ladder and desperately tried to hold it. But it was no use.

"Help! Help!" hollered Sir Spencer. "Aaaaaarrgh! NOOOOOOOOOOOO!"

The ladder, the dummy and Sir Spencer plummeted into the water with a tremendous SPLASH!

101

KNIGHTMARE

Algernon ran to help Sir Spencer out of the lake. As Sir Spencer sloshed on to the bank he seemed unharmed. But he was covered from head to toe in slime and mud.

"My new cloak!" he howled, spitting out a mouthful of frogspawn. "It's ruined!"

KNIGHTMARE

The High Steward cried "Disqualified!" but we hardly heard her above Sir Roland's roars of laughter. We had a hard job not laughing ourselves. "You failed on three counts," she went on. "One, bashing the lady's head on the rungs. Two, failure to bring the lady back safely. And three, receiving assistance from your squire. Sir Spencer, kindly leave the castle!"

"Bad luck, old bean!" said Sir Percy, trying not to grin.

"Hey, Spencer, that was epic!" guffawed Sir Roland. "An epic FAIL! *Hur-hur-hur!*"

The High Steward escorted the squelching Sir Spencer back to the boat. "Right, Sir Percy!" she said. "Your turn!"

In a split second Sir Percy's face switched from a smirk to a look of sheer panic.

"Come along!" said the High Steward impatiently. "We haven't got all day!"

Sir Percy sighed and slipped into the pavilion. After a minute or two I heard him cry, "Splendid! The very thing!" He then emerged with what looked like a sort of round table tucked under his arm.

"What's that, Sir Percy?" I asked. Peering more closely I saw that it was basically a wide metal hoop on four legs, with tough leather stretched tightly across the top. "Is it some kind of drum?"

"This is a *battle-bouncer*," smiled Sir Percy, placing it on the ground near the bottom of the tower. "A brand-new invention. I've seen them advertised in *Horse and Helm.* They save you the bother of scaling a castle wall. Instead you simply bounce up to the battlements. Neat, eh? Here goes! Three, two, one – Way-HAY!"

He leaped with both feet on to the battle-bouncer.

BOINGGGGG!

Everyone gasped as Sir Percy bounced about two metres sideways – into a large rose bush.

"Aaaargh!" he wailed. "Get me out!"

As Patchcoat and I ran to help I suddenly remembered reading that the new battle-bouncers had a few "teething problems". In other words, they were rubbish. Mind you, they looked fun, as long as you weren't in the middle of an actual battle. Or too fussy about where you landed.

Sir Roland's guffaws almost drowned out the sound of a fanfare of trumpets. Patchcoat and I stopped in our tracks as a pair of female heralds marched into the clearing. Right behind them was a tall woman. Her face was shaded by a hood.

"Your Royal Highness!" declared
the High Steward. "Welcome! I wasn't
expecting you."

It was the princess!

"Hello, Countess," she said. "I spotted
that rather soggy knight leaving and I
couldn't resist coming to watch the others.
Have I missed anything exciting?"

Was there something familiar about
that voice?

"You *could* say that, Your Royal
Highness," said the High Steward.

Sir Percy gave another squawk as he
tried to wriggle free of the bush.

"Good gracious! Who on earth is

that in my favourite rose bush?" said the princess. "He's wrecking all my blooms!"

"*That*," said the High Steward, "is Sir Percy the Proud."

At that very moment Sir Percy tumbled out of the rose bush, right at the feet of the princess.

She gasped. "*What* did you say his name was, Countess?" she asked.

"Sir Percy, Your Royal Highness," said the High Steward.

"*Sir Percy*," said the princess. "Well, well."

"Indeed so, Your Royal Highness!" shmoozed Sir Percy, struggling to his feet. "Have we had the pleasure of meeting before? How delightf—"

KNIGHTMARE

"Oh, we've met before all right," the princess cut him short. "But it certainly wasn't a pleasure. There was a bush involved *then*, too. And *you* said your name was Sir *Patrick*!"

The princess pulled down her hood.

I was right. I *had* heard her voice before. Princess Astra-Felicia was none other than the young woman Sir Percy had disastrously failed to rescue the day before!

Sir Percy went rather pale. "Ah – er – well, yes – um – ha ha!" he spluttered. "Well, I'm sure we can – um – let bygones be bygones, eh, Your Royal Highness? No hard feelings, and all that? What do you say?"

The princess glowered at him. "You've got two minutes to get off my island!" she hissed. "*That's* what I say."

"But – but what about the challenge?" wailed Sir Percy. "Don't I get another go?"

"Certainly not," said the High Steward. "You know the rules. One go only. Guards! Escort these gentlemen to the boat."

"And if you set foot on my island again I'll lock you up at the top of my highest tower," cried the princess. "And throw the key into the lake!"

"I've won! I've won!" bellowed Sir

KNIGHTMARE

Roland as the guards arrived. "I'm gonna marry the princess! Hur-hur!"

"Well done, Sir Roland!" simpered Walter. "My master's just the right husband for you, Your Royal Highness. And I'm the *perfect* squire."

He smirked at me nastily. I gave him a furious glare in return.

"Not so fast!" said the princess, looking Sir Roland up and down. "I need to think before I decide if I want to marry you or not. I will tell you my decision at sunset. High Steward, see that Sir Roland waits here until I send for him!"

And with that Princess Astra-Felicia swept past us into the castle.

Chapter Seven

Frock Shock

"Go home? Nonsense, dear boy!" said Sir Percy. "I'm not giving up that easily. If Roland ends up marrying the princess I'll never hear the end of it. No, there is *another* way to the princess's heart."

"Really, Sir Percy?" I said.

"Yes, Cedric. You see, I have a little *back-up plan*."

KNIGHTMARE

Sir Percy, Patchcoat and I were standing a little way from the ferry that had brought us back to the town. Sir Percy checked no one was looking, then fished a small bottle of strange red liquid out of his saddlebag. "Here, Cedric. I'd like you to look after this for me."

"What's that then?" asked Patchcoat, giving me a wink. "More tummy potion?"

"Oh no. My tummy has been fine since my last little – um – *episode*," said Sir Percy. "This is the *real* reason I nipped into the alchemist's. It's a *love* potion."

"A *love potion*?" I said.

"Indeed," said Sir Percy. "When the princess drinks it, she will fall madly in

love with the first person she sees. All
I have to do is make sure that the first
person she sees is *me*. The alchemist said
that just a few drops should do the trick."

"But isn't that ... cheating, Sir
Percy?" I said before I could stop myself.

"*Cheating*, Cedric?" said Sir Percy.
"Certainly not. The effects of the potion
only last a short time. But that will be
enough to allow the princess a proper
chance to, um, appreciate my merits.
Unless, of course, you'd *prefer* Sir Roland
to marry her?"

"Well, no, I suppose not."

"Excellent," said Sir Percy. "Now we
must return at once to the castle!"

"But it's only two o'clock in the afternoon," I said. "Sunset's not till eight."

"So we must make hay while the sun shines, Cedric," said Sir Percy. "The longer we have, the more chance there is of success!"

We walked back to the jetty. The twin sisters eyed us suspiciously.

"'Ere," said one. "We thought you'd been sent 'ome."

"Like that other gentleman," said her sister. "The wet one."

"Oh, ah, I – I forgot something," said Sir Percy. "I'm – er – just nipping back to the castle to fetch it."

"No way," said one of the sisters. "Clear off."

KNIGHTMARE

"Of course, of course!" said Sir Percy breezily. He gave me and Patchcoat a rather obvious wink. Subtlety isn't always Sir Percy's strong point. *Now* what was he up to? "But first you might want to catch that chap climbing through your cottage window."

The sisters looked at each other in alarm, then turned and ran to their cottage.

"Quickly, into the boat!" hissed Sir Percy. "Grab the oars and row!"

We landed on the edge of a wood on the other side of the island from the castle and tied the boat to an overhanging tree.

KNIGHTMARE

"Goody!" said Sir Percy. "Now, how can we sneak into the castle without being seen?"

"Through the kitchens?" I said.

"Precisely what I was going to suggest," said Sir Percy.

We slunk through the trees towards the castle, being careful to avoid the clearing where the challenge had taken place. We reached the kitchen yard without bumping into the High Steward or Sir Roland.

Stewie the goat bleated as we crept across the yard. We froze. But nobody came.

I peeked nervously around the kitchen door. "All clear!" I said.

KNIGHTMARE

We sneaked through the kitchen.
A door at the far end led into a wood-
panelled corridor. All seemed to be going
well. Then we heard footsteps!

We ducked back into the kitchen. The
footsteps got louder.

"Into the privy, quick!" said Patchcoat.

We dived into the servants' privy just
as someone entered the kitchen.

"Now, where did Peggy put that
blinkin' broom?" said a voice. It sounded
like one of the castle servants. "I know!
Maybe it's in the privy."

In a panic the three of us dived for cover
behind the princess's dresses. A split second
later, the loo door opened.

"Ah, there it is!" said the servant. I held
my breath as her hand grabbed the broom
that was leaning against the wall about a
foot from my head. She shut the door and
we waited till she had walked away.

"This is impossible," sighed Sir Percy.
"Even if we actually manage to get out of
the kitchen *and* avoid the High Steward,
one of the servants is bound to see us and
raise the alarm."

I popped up from behind a fine satin evening gown.

"Well," I grinned. "There is *one* way for you to sneak through the castle unnoticed, Sir Percy."

I nodded at all the fancy frocks.

"Blithering breastplates!" said Sir Percy. "My dear Cedric, are you mad? Surely you are not suggesting that *I*, Sir Percy the Proud, famed throughout the land as a shining example of knightly manhood, should resort to wearing – a *dress*?"

"It's only an idea, Sir Percy," I said. "But they'll hear you coming a mile off if you go clanking through the castle in your armour."

"Hmm," Sir Percy frowned. "I suppose you do have a point…"

"And remember that bit in *The Song of Percy* where you dressed as a slave girl?" Patchcoat piped up. "And single-handedly captured a ship full of pirates?"

"Erm – er… "

"How does it go again?" said Patchcoat. "*Hail, Sir Percy, brave and wise, the greatest master of disguise!*"

"Ah… Oh, well, of course, if you put it like *that*," said Sir Percy. "There's – um – no harm in seeing if any of these frocks happens to be my size, eh?"

Sir Percy started to rummage among the princess's wardrobe.

"Nice one, Ced!" whispered Patchcoat. "I can't wait to see Sir Percy in a dress!"

"And well done for quoting *The Song of Percy*," I said. "I can't remember that bit at all."

"Not surprising," said Patchcoat. "I made it up."

"Here we are!" said Sir Percy. He held up an expensive-looking pink silk frock with a matching pointy headdress. "Everything else is too short so this'll just have to do. Cedric, help me out of my armour and into this dress."

"Yes, Sir Percy," I said. I tried not to smile. A bloke in a frock! I couldn't imagine anything more hilarious.

"And while you're doing that, Ced, I'll find something for the pair of us," said Patchcoat.

"Huh?" I said. "What do you mean?"

"Well, there's no point only *one* of us being disguised as a woman, is there?" he chuckled. "Now, I'm sure I spotted a few serving-maids' dresses somewhere."

I shook my head in horror.

"Oooh no," I said firmly. "Don't even think about it, Patchcoat. No, no, no, no, no. I am NOT, repeat *NOT* wearing a dress. Absolutely not. I refuse. Point blank. No. Nope. No way."

"There!" said Patchcoat, adjusting the maid's cap on my head. "You make a smashing girl, Ced!"

He pursed his lips and pretended to try and kiss me on my cheek.

"Oi, gerroff!" I said. "And why do these bodices have to be so tight?"

"Count yourself lucky," said Patchcoat, hitching up his skirt and scratching his legs. "These woolly knickers are as itchy as heck!"

"Now, stop messing around, you two,"

said Sir Percy, swishing one of the princess's plush velvet cloaks round his shoulders. "We had better get out of here before somebody else comes. Cedric, do you have the potion?"

I patted the pocket of my apron. "Yes, Sir Percy."

"Excellent. Now, I'd better just check my disguise *one* last time."

He held up a mirror. Actually he looked rather good in the dress. Apart from his stubbly chin and hairy chest.

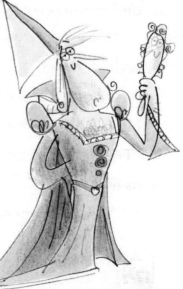

"Splendid!" he declared, putting down the mirror. "How poor old Spence would have loved this!" he chortled. "*Such* a pity he had to go home!"

"Shh!" said Patchcoat suddenly.

We froze. Someone had entered the kitchen and started clattering and clonking about. Then we heard more footsteps, hurrying this time.

"You, girl!" snapped a voice. "What are you doing?"

It was the High Steward!

"Just takin' Her Highness some lemonade, ma'am," said a familiar voice.

It was Peggy. My heart missed a beat. With all the excitement, obviously.

"Ah, very good," said the High Steward. "Have you seen any *males*?"

"Males, ma'am?" said Peggy.

"Yes, males," said the High Steward. "The head gardener says she saw some *males* lurking in the trees near the kitchens. And one of them was a knight!"

Uh-oh.

"D'you think it was that big one, ma'am?" said Peggy. "The one who looks like a bear?"

"No. It definitely wasn't him," said the High Steward. "From the gardener's description it sounds more like the *pompous* one."

"Charming!" muttered Sir Percy.

"Oh, then that means his squire's still here, too!" said Peggy cheerfully.

My face went a bit warm again.

"Yes, and that jester fellow," said the High Steward. "The gardener said there were *three* of them. I will tell the guards to search the grounds. Then I must inform the princess. When we catch them we'll have all three locked in the high tower!"

At that moment a thunderous knocking echoed through the castle.

"Now what?" sighed the High Steward.

"Sounds like the front door, ma'am," said Peggy. "Shall I go and answer it?"

"Yes, please," said the High Steward. "I hope it's not that big hairy knight

again. He's *so* impatient. Keeps asking if
Her Highness has made up her mind yet!"

We heard Peggy and the High Steward
leave the kitchen. Then we slipped out of
our hiding place.

"Look!" said Patchcoat, as we crept
along the corridor. "The servants' stairs!
I bet they lead straight to the princess's
private quarters."

"Hold on," I said suddenly. "I've just
thought of something!"

I dashed back into the kitchen and
returned with the tray of lemonade.

"Really, Cedric," said Sir Percy. "This is
no time for refreshments!"

"It's not for us, Sir Percy," I said.

"I thought we could put the love potion in it."

"Ah ... indeed!" said Sir Percy. "The very thing I was about to suggest myself." *Yeah, right.* "On we go, then. Cedric, I shall give you the honour of leading the way!"

Chapter Eight

Hide and Shriek

We tiptoed up the narrow servants' stairs
and came out on a grand, oak-panelled
landing. It was lined with rich tapestries
and paintings of formidable women
wearing tiaras and old-fashioned dresses –
the princess's ancestors, by the look of them.

Patchcoat pointed to a large door
decorated with a gold crown.

"Her Highness's private quarters,
I reckon," said Patchcoat.

"Can you hear anything, Cedric?"
whispered Sir Percy.

I put down the tray and stuck my ear
to the keyhole.

"All quiet, Sir Percy," I said.

But I spoke too soon. At the far end of
the landing was another set of stairs, much
grander than the ones we'd come up. And
someone was climbing them in a hurry!

There was no time to hide. Patchcoat
and I just managed to swivel Sir Percy
round so that he was facing the other way
when the High Steward appeared at the
top of the stairs.

KNIGHTMARE

Patchcoat and I bobbed hasty curtsies and looked firmly at the ground. I guessed we had five seconds at the most before the High Steward called for the guards. So we were surprised by what came next.

"Your Highness! Your Highness!" the High Steward said breathlessly, looking towards Sir Percy. "Ah! I see you've changed for dinner. Are you all right?"

KNIGHTMARE

Sir Percy had the sense to say nothing and just nod vigorously.

"I'm glad to hear it," the High Steward said. "There appear to be several intruders loose on the island. And *male* ones at that! The guards are searching for them. Has Your Highness heard anything?"

Sir Percy shook his head wildly.

Any more overacting like that and you'll definitely blow our cover! I thought.

And then Patchcoat did something completely crazy.

"I knows where they is, ma'am!" he cried in a squeaky girly voice.

I felt Sir Percy flinch. What was Patchcoat playing at?

"Really, girl?" said the High Steward. "Where?"

Patchcoat ran across the landing and pointed to the servants' stairs.

"Down there, ma'am!" he squeaked. "I think I 'eard someone 'iding in the servants' privy, ma'am!"

"Good gracious!" gasped the High Steward.

"I'll show yer if yer likes, ma'am!" said Patchcoat. "Foller me!"

Patchcoat disappeared down the stairs.

"Aha! Now we've got them! Wait for me, girl!" cried the High Steward. "Will you kindly excuse me, Your Highness?"

Sir Percy nodded eagerly and the High

KNIGHTMARE

Steward dashed after Patchcoat.

I sighed with relief.

"Phew!" I said. "But I don't know how long he'll be able to distract her for. So we'd better get a move on."

"Indeed!" said Sir Percy. "In you go, Cedric. You have nothing to fear. I am right behind you!"

I slowly opened the door to the princess's private quarters. We found ourselves in a splendid parlour with a roaring fire and several large comfy chairs. There were a couple of doors leading into other parts of the private quarters. I guessed one of them probably led to the princess's bedchamber.

KNIGHTMARE

I put down the tray of lemonade on a
low table near the fire.

"Now pass me the potion, Cedric," said
Sir Percy, rubbing his hands together in
excitement.

"Yes, Sir Percy."

I took the bottle of love potion from
my apron and handed it to Sir Percy. He
pulled out the cork while I poured a glass
of lemonade.

"Excellent!" said Sir Percy. "Here goes."

"Just a few drops, remember," I said.

"Indeed," said Sir Percy. "It's very powerful stuff."

He dripped a small amount of the potion into the glass of lemonade – just as we heard footsteps out on the landing. The door handle rattled.

Sir Percy was so startled he accidentally shook about half the bottle into the glass.

"Bother! Oh well. The longer the potion lasts, the longer I have to win her over. Quick, make yourself scarce, Cedric! As soon as Her Highness has drunk the potion I shall appear! We must ensure I am the first person she sees."

KNIGHTMARE

He quickly scuttled off and hid behind a tapestry hanging on the far wall. I flung myself under a long bench on one side of the door.

From my hiding place I could hear a commotion on the landing. There seemed to be *two* people at the door. One was Peggy. The other sounded a bit deep and gruff for the princess.

"No!" I heard Peggy say. "You can't go in there, sir!"

"Rubbish!" said the gruff voice. "I've waited long enough. Outta my way!"

The door burst open and someone stomped past me across the room. I dared to peek and saw a pair of legs striding towards the table with the tray on it. Then I heard the clink of glass followed by a rather unladylike slurping.

I stared at the legs again. They were wearing black armour.

Black armour?

And then I spotted a pink silk dress slip out from behind the tapestry.

"No, Sir Percy!" I shouted, crawling from my hiding place. "Stop!"

It was too late.

"Your Highness!" he declared. "It is I, Sir Percy the Proud. Your future husb— AARRGH!"

Sir Percy stared in horror at the person who had just walked into the chamber.

KNIGHTMARE

It wasn't the princess. It was Sir Roland!

"Ah! Oh! I – um – hello, Sir Roland!"
he babbled. "What an – um – an
unexpected pleasure! I was – er – just – um
– I mean, I – I can explain…"

KNIGHTMARE

Sir Roland's jaw dropped. He stared at Sir Percy in utter amazement. Uh-oh. Things did NOT look good for Sir Percy. Any second now, Sir Roland was going to blast him with the biggest torrent of ridicule. Once the story got out Sir Percy would never, EVER live it down.

But Sir Roland didn't say a word. His eyes had a strange, glazed look. I thought it was just the shock of seeing Sir Percy in a dress. But then I noticed the lemonade glass on the tray. It was empty.

That slurping sound… Oh no!

A weird dreamy smile started to spread across Sir Roland's face. He raised both arms and started to move towards Sir Percy.

"My beloved!" he sighed soppily.
"Come here!" Sir Roland puckered up his
lips and lurched at Sir Percy.

"Look, let's be sensible, Roland, old
chap!" Sir Percy whimpered. He grabbed a
chair to fend off his besotted arch-enemy.
"W-why don't we j-just sit down and talk
about it, eh?"

"Aw, don't be shy!" simpered Sir Roland, whacking the chair aside. "Your darling Rolykins only wants a little kiss!"

Rolykins?

Sir Percy dropped the chair and started to run.

"C-Cedric, help!" he shrieked, stumbling over his skirts as Sir Roland chased him round the chamber.

"Hur-hur! Playing hard to get, are we?" cackled Sir Roland. "You little minx! Let's have a cuddle!"

I made a rather feeble attempt to grab Sir Roland but he was too quick for me.

"Aargh!"

RRRIP!

Poor Sir Percy had tripped on his hem, tearing a hole in the dress and tumbling headlong into a corner of the chamber.

"Now I've got you, my lovely!" sighed Sir Roland. He puckered up his lips again.

Sir Percy was trapped.

"Cedric!" he wailed, as Sir Roland leaned forward to try to plant a great beardy smacker on his cheek. "For goodness' sake! Do something!"

I had to act fast. In a flash I saw that Sir Roland was standing on one end of a small rug. I bent down and yanked the other end of it with all my might. Sir Roland gave a great bellow of surprise as

he lost his balance and toppled in a heap.
Luckily my master rolled out of the way
just in time.

"Hurry, Sir Percy!" I cried. "Now's your
chance!"

Sir Percy didn't need telling twice. With
a squawk he hitched up his dress, sprinted
across the room in terror, and leaped for
cover behind a large couch. His pink pointy
hat flew off and landed nearby.

"Ungh? Where am I?" said Sir Roland,
groggily getting to his feet. "What
happened, boy?"

"Er – I think you tripped, Sir Roland!"
I said, desperately buying time. Out of the
corner of my eye I saw Sir Percy's hand

creeping from behind the couch towards the pointy hat.

The goofy, dreamy look came back into Sir Roland's eyes.

"Ah, yes, I remember," he gurgled softly. "Where is she? Where's my sweetheart?"

He scanned the room. Sir Percy's hand grabbed the hat and shot back behind the couch in the nick of time.

"Oh, she – she's left, Sir Roland," I stammered.

"*Left?*" quailed Sir Roland. He began to sob. "Waah! My beloved has left me! Waahaaaaaah!"

"She went that way!" I flung open the door to the chamber. "She – she went... downstairs!"

Sir Roland ran out of the door and down the landing, hollering, "Come back, my darling! Come back to your Rolykins!"

I quickly shut the door after him. "You can come out now, Sir Percy!" I hissed.

"Phew!" said Sir Percy, as he crawled from behind the couch. "Really, Cedric, you might have got rid of him sooner. He came so close to kissing me I could smell what he had for lunch!"

"Er, sorry, Sir Percy," I said. *And next time I will let him kiss you, you ungrateful so-and-so. Whose idea was this stupid love*

potion anyway?

"So, where were we?" said Sir Percy. "Pass me the potion."

"Really, Sir Percy?" I blurted. "Don't you think we should just get out of here? Somebody's bound to have heard Sir Roland!"

"Precisely, Cedric," said Sir Percy. "And at this very moment the entire castle will be chasing after him. It's the perfect distraction." He poured out another glass of lemonade and tipped a large dose of potion into it. "No point in holding back now we've seen what this stuff can do, eh?"

But suddenly we heard footsteps approaching the chamber. As they came

closer I recognized the voices of the High
Steward – and the princess!

There was no time to hide. Then I
spotted a narrow door next to one of the
tapestries. From a distance it looked like it
was just part of the panelling. But close up
I saw that it had a small doorknob and a
little brass sign:

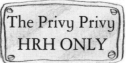

The Privy Privy
HRH ONLY

"Quick, Sir Percy, in here!" I hissed.

We crammed ourselves into the royal
loo just as the chamber door opened.

"What on earth is going on, Countess?"
I heard the princess say. "What's Sir
Roland doing in the castle? I ordered him

to wait outside!"

"Indeed, Your Highness," said the High
Steward. "But young Peggy answered
the door and there he was with that
weedy squire of his. She managed to keep
out his squire, but Sir Roland barged in
demanding to see you!"

"Me?" said the princess. "It's not *me*
he's after. He just ran straight past me
jabbering on about some *other* woman. Men
are so fickle! I didn't fancy him anyway,
great hairy brute. Who do you think he's
after? Surely not one of the servants?"

"Who else? There are no other ladies
in the castle," declared the High Steward.
"Hold on. Maybe it was that girl who

locked me in the servants' privy. Aha! Yes, that's it! She tricked me so she could meet Sir Roland!"

Nice one, Patchcoat!

"What? A *servant* locked you in the *privy*?" gasped the princess.

"Yes, Your Highness. She was with you when I saw you earlier. After you'd changed your dress. Though I see you've changed back again."

"I don't know *who* you saw earlier," said the princess, "but it definitely wasn't me. I've worn this dress all day."

"Really, Your Highness?" said the High Steward. "How very odd."

"Indeed," said the princess. "Anyway,

how did you get out of the privy?"

"The cook eventually heard me calling," said the High Steward.

"Well, we'd better catch Sir Roland *and* that girl who locked you up," said the princess. "Now, here's what we'll do…"

The princess must have turned away because I didn't catch the rest. I just heard the High Steward saying, "Very good, Your Highness," and then footsteps leaving the chamber. I guessed the High Steward had left the princess alone in the chamber.

I pressed my ear to the privy door and heard a slight chink and a glugging noise.

I turned to Sir Percy. "I think the princess is drinking the potion!"

KNIGHTMARE

But then I heard a voice splutter "Ugh!" followed by footsteps rapidly heading in our direction!

"Sir Percy! She's coming this way!" I hissed.

"What?" panicked Sir Percy. "Hide, Cedric! Whatever happens the princess must see *me* first!"

Hide? In a loo? In a panic I managed to squeeze myself to one side of the door just as the person outside flung it open.

"This lemonade is disgusting!" she said. "The only place for it is down the privy!"

But the person clutching the lemonade jug wasn't the princess at all. It was the High Steward!

Chapter Nine
Castle Kiss Chase

"Good heavens!" screeched the High Steward. "Sir Percy! What on earth is the meaning of ... of..."

She stopped. I slid out from behind the door to see her eyes going all goofy and soppy.

Uh-oh.

"Your S-Stewardship!" stuttered

Sir Percy. "I – I – can explain… You see, I thought you were the princess…"

"The princess? Don't worry, my darling, Her Highness won't disturb us! She has gone to speak to the guards about some *naughty* knights," she said dreamily. "Oh, Sir Percy! You look so *handsome* in that dress!" The High Steward pushed Sir Percy on to the loo seat, plumped herself on his lap and threw her arms round his neck. "Now, Sir Percy, how about a tiny little peck?"

"Oh – er – m-my dear lady!" he stammered. "There appears to be – to be – some mistake!"

"Mistake? Oh, you *are* a joker,

KNIGHTMARE

Sir Percy!" warbled the High Steward. "I knew it when I first saw you! Imagine the fun we'll have when we're married!"

"Married?" squawked Sir Percy. "Cedric, do something!"

He wriggled frantically. But the High Steward didn't budge.

"What an excellent game, my darling!" she trilled. "What shall we play next?"

I saw my chance. "Er – hide-and-seek!" I said. "Sir Percy loves hide-and-seek, don't you, Sir Percy?"

"Do I, Cedric?" he moaned feebly.

"Yes, Sir Percy," I said, desperately trying to get him to twig. "It's your *favourite* game, *remember*?"

"Oh, Sir Percy, *I* adore hide-and-seek, too!" said the High Steward. "Let's play, my darling, let's!"

"Sir Percy especially loves to *hide* first," I said. "*Don't* you, Sir Percy?"

"Ah! Yes! Yes!" he said, finally seeing what I was getting at. "Hide first! Yes, indeed! Most definitely!"

"Well, go on then, my beloved Percy-
wercy!" chortled the High Steward,
climbing off Sir Percy's lap. "You hide in
the chamber while I stay here and count."

"To a hundred, mind!" said Sir Percy.
"And no peeking!"

"Very well, my darling. Off you go!" She
blew Sir Percy a kiss. Then she shut her eyes
and started to count, "One, two, three…"

We slipped out of the Privy Privy
and tiptoed across the chamber. We
carefully opened the door to the landing
and were checking the coast was clear
when Patchcoat appeared at the top of the
servants' stairs.

"Wotcher!" he said. "Sorry I took so long. I kept having to dodge all these castle guards. The bad news is I heard one of them saying they'd found the boat."

"Bother!" said Sir Percy. "We'll need another way of getting off the island. But whatever we do, we can't stay here. The High Steward will have nearly counted to a hundred!"

"Eh?" said Patchcoat. "But I locked her in the servants' loo!"

"We know," I said, heading for the servants' stairs. "But the cook let her out."

"Oh well," said Patchcoat. "At least it bought you some time to do the potion business. Did it work?"

"Er, yes … and no," I said. "I'll explain on the way. We need to get out of here without the High Steward or Sir Roland seeing Sir Percy!"

"*Sir Roland?*" gasped Patchcoat. "You mean *he's* in the castle?"

I briefly told Patchcoat what had happened as we dashed down the stairs to the kitchen. We reached the bottom – only to run right into Peggy.

"Afternoon, Your Highness!" she said, curtsying to Sir Percy.

"Peggy!" I said. "It's Sir Percy. And me, Cedric!"

Peggy looked up and gasped. "Gracious me, so it is!" she said. "You do look funny,

Cedric! Why are you dressed up like that?"

"We have to get off the island," I said. "Please will you help us? If we're caught we'll all be locked in the tower!"

"Or worse," pleaded Sir Percy. "If the High Steward or Sir Roland catch me first!"

"I'm sorry, sir," said Peggy. "I mean, I'd really *like* to –" she glanced at me – "but if old Stew... – er – the High Steward found out, I'd lose my job."

"Please, my dear girl!" whined Sir Percy. "There's no time to lose!"

"Oh, well, I'd hate to see you locked in the tower." Peggy smiled at me and I felt that funny warm feeling come back to my face. "And if we're careful no one'll see us.

So yes, I *will* help you. I know where
there's an old rowing boat. Cook uses it to
go fishing. Come on!"

"Hold on!" said Sir Percy suddenly. "It
won't do to travel home dressed like this.
Cedric, fetch my armour. But hurry!"

Patchcoat and I dashed into the
servants' privy. Patchcoat hastily gathered
up his clothes and mine while I retrieved
Sir Percy's armour.

Making sure no one was in sight, Peggy
led the way out of the kitchen and into
the woods. Sir Percy huffed as his pink
dress caught on the brambles and thorns.
At least he didn't have to stumble along
carrying about half a ton of metal.

We finally came to a dense bit of
woodland away from the castle. "There it
is," said Peggy, pointing to an old rowing
boat under some bushes.

"Splendid!" said Sir Percy. "Now let's
get out of here!"

Peggy, Patchcoat and I started to pull

the boat down to the shore. Suddenly we heard voices nearby.

"Oh, Sir Roland!" whined Walter. "I wondered where you were. That silly girl shut the door in my face! Did you see the princess, Sir Roland? Are you going to marry her?"

"Princess? Don't be silly, Walter!" roared the reply. "There's only one woman I'm interested in. And, oh joy! There she is! Come here, my darling!"

To Sir Percy's horror, Sir Roland suddenly lumbered out of the bushes towards him — with Walter in hot pursuit.

"Arrgh! Help!" yelped Sir Percy.

He looked about for somewhere to run.

"A tree, Sir Percy!" I cried.

Sir Percy scrambled frantically up the nearest tree. But he wasn't quite fast enough. Sir Roland grabbed his dress and started to pull.

"Come to your Rolykins, my darling!" bellowed Sir Roland. "Just one little peck for your Rolykins!"

"Stop, Sir Roland!" wailed Walter, trying to pull him off Sir Percy. "What are you doing?" He turned and glared at me. "You're behind this, Fatbottom, I know it! What have you done to my master?"

And then someone else appeared out of the bushes.

"Coo-eee! Found you, you naughty

Percy-wercy! Come down from that tree and give us a kiss!"

The High Steward!

"CEDRIC!" shrieked Sir Percy, as she, too, grabbed hold of his dress.

"My word!" gasped Peggy. "Have they both gone bonkers?"

"Er – long story," I said. "I'll tell you later. Let's help my master first!"

Walter, Patchcoat, Peggy and I all tried to drag Sir Roland and the High Steward off. But I reckon the potion must have given the pair of them superhuman strength. They just clung on even harder.

"Mine!" wailed Sir Roland.

"Mine!" whined the High Steward.

"Good grief!" cried another voice. As things couldn't get any worse, the princess strode out of the bushes followed by several guards. "Sir Roland! Countess! What is the meaning of this? Why is Sir Percy still here? *And why* is he wearing my best frock?"

"Help!" cried Sir Percy. "I can't hold on much longer!"

RRRRIIIIPP!

The pulling was too much for Sir Percy's dress. With a horrible tearing sound, the whole lower part suddenly came away.

"My dress!" cried the princess, as all six of us went flying backwards – and landed in the lake with a terrific SPLASH!

The guards ran to help us out.

"What's going on?" said Sir Roland.

"Where am I?" said the High Steward.

It must have been the shock of the cold water. The love potion had suddenly worn off.

"Yikes," I muttered to Patchcoat, as I shook the stinking pond-slime from my clothes. "The princess is going to be SO mad!"

"I'm not so sure about that," chuckled Patchcoat. "Look!"

Her Royal Highness was in hysterics, with tears of laughter running down her face. And then I saw Sir Percy.

"Now look here!" he said. "Will

someone *please* help me down?"

He was still dangling from the tree, wearing only half a dress. And no wonder the princess was laughing.

His bare bottom was on display for all to see.

KNIGHTMARE

"Sir Percy was really lucky!" said Patchcoat.

"Lucky?" I said. "He was *so* embarrassed!" It was going to take a *long* time to get the picture of Sir Percy's bottom out of my head.

"Yeah, but if he hadn't given the princess such a good laugh she *definitely* would have locked him in the tower," said Patchcoat. "And us, too, probably. Sir Percy was lucky she let him go as long as he promised to pay for *two* new dresses."

It was early evening and we were almost home. Peggy had seen us off with a basket of food that she'd managed to sneak out of the kitchen of Noman Castle. Sir Percy was in front on Prancelot. He seemed a lot happier now he was back in his armour.

"But there's still Sir Roland," I said. "He's bound to tell everyone what a ninny Sir Percy made of himself. He'll be the laughing stock of the whole kingdom!"

"I wouldn't be so sure about that," said Patchcoat. "After all, Sir Percy wasn't the one chasing around after a knight in a dress. I think Sir Roland might keep rather quiet about the whole business."

We rode through the castle gate and pulled up at the stables just as Margaret came striding out of the kitchen.

"Welcome 'ome!" she said. "You must

173

all be 'ungry after your journey. I've got a lovely cabbage and gizzard tart on the go!"

As I got down off the cart I felt something fall out of my pocket.

"Oh, you dropped something, Master Cedric," she said. "What is it? Beetroot sauce? Let's have a taste."

I turned round to see Margaret pick up a small bottle, pull off the cork and take a swig.

"No, stop!" I called.

But it was too late. Margaret stared at me. Her eyes went all googly.

"Oh, Master Cedric," she said. "Come 'ere and give us a kiss!"

Uh-oh!

Have you read?